Cooking With Daddy

Corinthia A. Myrick

Copyright © 2018 by Corinthia A. Myrick

Written by Corinthia A. Myrick

Illustrated by Mary K. Biswas

All rights reserved. No part of this book may be used or reproduced in any manner whatsoever without the prior written permission of the author.

This book is dedicated to Carole Denise Wilson Reed (May 7, 1960- February 22, 2018), who provided the eighth seasoning: Vision.

Cooking With Daddy

"Good Morning princess Kenya!" Daddy said as he jumped onto Kenya's bed, causing her to wake up.

"Daddy," she mumbled. "Why can't you just wake me up like a regular person, it's too early!"

Daddy began to tickle Kenya until tears fell down her face from laughing. She finally gave in and jumped out of the bed to fight back.

"Whoa!" Daddy exclaimed, "I hope you're about to do your hair and treat that bad case of dragon breath!"

Kenya smirked. "Daddy, are you done joking around?"

"For now!" he said smiling gently.

"Kenya, what do you have a taste for tonight?"

"I want pot roast and rice, covered with brown pepper gravy, turnip greens, sweet honey corn bread and some ice tea."

"You want all of that?" Daddy asked teasingly.

"Yes!"

"Well, let's go to the store. But first, you must wash up, brush those beautiful teeth, and bring a brush so we can do your hair."

"Yes sir!" Kenya said.

"Where are we going?"

"It's a surprise," Daddy said.

They pulled up to a huge building.

"The sign says, Farmers Market. What is that daddy?"

"Let's go find out."

Daddy held Kenya's hand as they walked into the Farmers Market.

"Daddy, look at all the vegetables!" Kenya said with excitement. Daddy picked Kenya up so she could get a bunch of turnip greens from the colorful vegetable stand.

"Perfect," Kenya said.

"Kenya, I'm going to get a few more things and we can go back home to cook our meal."

Once they made it home, Kenya helped daddy unpack the car and put away the groceries. She then washed her hands to help prepare the meal.

"Well Kenya, let's get started. You're going to be my little helper today!"

Kenya's eyes beamed with excitement as she went to get her own apron and chef hat.

She immediately ran back to daddy yelling, "I'M READY, I'M READY!"

"Kenya, remember the rules," Daddy said with a stern look.

"Yes Daddy, I remember the rules." Kenya said.
"One, do not touch the stove or burner."

"Two, do not use any knives."

"Three, do not attend to any other task without being supervised."

"Perfect," Daddy said as he gathered the seasonings for the meal.

As Daddy seasoned the roast, he seemed excited.

"Kenya, do you know what people called me back in the day?"

"Mr. 7 Seasonings! How could I forget?" Kenya exclaimed

"That's right, I fed a thousand people a day, and still do!" Daddy said.

"I use pepper, Season All, garlic salt, onion powder, Terry's Seasoning, a pinch of salt and the last ingredient is a secret."

"Daddy, tell me the secret!" Kenya begged.

"Kenya, what good is a secret if it's told?" he said.

"No good I suppose... but what if we switched the rules so it's just a secret between you and me?"

Daddy finally looked up from chopping onions, wiped his watering eyes and said, "You are hard to bargain with young lady! I'll tell you when we're finished cooking."

"Do you pinky promise?" Kenya asked as she stuck her pinky right between his eyes. "Yes, I promise," Daddy said.

They connected their pinkies and he kissed her cheek.

"The roast should cook slowly for the next 2 ½ hours," he said. Kenya stepped far away from the stove as she watched her daddy open the fiery oven and put the roast in.

Once that was done, they started making the squash.

"Daddy, I don't like squash!" Kenya said.

"Well you'll like squash after we finish making THIS casserole!"

"If you don't like it, I will wash dishes for the rest of the week, but if you do like it, you're going to help me in the garden next week." he said.

"It's a bet!" Kenya said as she mixed the cheese and peppers in the casserole dish. As she worked on the casserole, Daddy dropped the turnips into the large pot.

Soon, the house was filled with a delightful smell. The kitchen was steaming, the turnips were simmering, the roast was baking, and the casserole was rising. It had been almost two hours. The only thing left to do was make the rice, gravy, and sweet cornbread.

They sat at the table and then blessed the food. Everything was delicious, even the squash casserole.

Despite losing the bet, Kenya was delighted she would get to spend more time with her amazing daddy while growing a green thumb.

Suddenly, Kenya remembered...

"Daddy, what's the seventh secret seasoning?"

"The seventh seasoning is love."

THE END

Made in the USA
Middletown, DE
30 October 2023

40979354R00018